A CHRISTMAS STORY

WITH

CLIFFORD PRIDEAUX

(1902-1963)

BY

A A PRIDEAUX

A CIP catalogue record for this title is

Available from the British Library.

ISBN 978-0-9930676-5-5

www.paganuspublishing.co.uk

First published in 2014

Paganus Publishing

Ruthin

Wales

Paganus Publishing

I am dedicating this book to my Grandma and Grandad

STORY DESCRIPTION

A Christmas Story is about my grandma and grandad. Christmas was always a special time for Grandad Clifford. The Christmas magic ran through his veins from the first day. Clifford was a kind man, but also a mystical one. Even after his death, he has visited his family on many occasions. I think of him as a hermit character, cloaked and walking with a long staff. He appeared in his role of Clifford for only 60 years before he returned to being the hermit.
A A Prideaux.

In this chapter from the Prideaux history series, the reader will learn something of Clifford. A Christmas Story gives the reader an idea of the times prior to the Great War for those with no money and no property. What the family had, was their love for each other and that love cannot be exaggerated.

A A Prideaux has written about each of her Prideaux ancestors from 1040 to the present day. She has traced every one of them through research and discovered where and how they lived. A A Prideaux has travelled miles in this search. She has old books, family documents and stories which have helped her in the conclusions drawn. Clifford Prideaux and her mother were responsible for setting the fire in her soul that turned into a Prideaux obsession.

A Christmas Story is one of her fictionalised tales which draw on known facts. In this case, the story is written with personal experience of the author. This Clifford Prideaux (1902-1963) story takes us to Leeds and a tiny stone cottage full of love and warmth. We travel through time to the end of his life and the effect it had on his wife, the woman A A was named after, Agnes Prideaux.

More information can be found on her website. www.aaprideaux.com

Contents

A CHRISTMAS STORY

Christmas Day of 1902 was a special day for the Prideaux family who lived in Burniston Place.

No 7 was exactly like its neighbours, a back to back, two up and one down terraced property.

Burniston Place was situated off Elland Road in Leeds and consisted of eight properties facing each other, four on either side. The odd numbers were on the left and the even numbers on the right. At the end of the court, was the shared toilet and midden which completed the C shape. Burniston Place was on the corner of Elland Road on the north side. Elland Road moved west from New Princess Street in the centre of Leeds.

Two steps led to each house door from the narrow flagged pavement and the cobbled street sloped to the middle. Here, a channel took the waste water to the drain at the midden and toilet.

Burniston Place was occupied by some of the very poor of Leeds who worked hard at making their low wages feed and clothe their families.

But they weren't paupers and were proud people.

On this Christmas morning, Georgie Prideaux was wakened by a noise from the bedroom he shared with his eight year old brother Arthur, seven year old sister Annie and 2 year old sister Jane. His parents slept in the bed at the other side of the room. A curtain drawn across the middle of the room, gave a small amount of privacy.

Georgie could hear his parents whispering to each other. He hoped he wasn't going to have to listen to the heavy breathing and bouncing again. He turned his head and forced it into the pillow. He put his arm over the upper ear and pressed down hard. Georgie had learned that this was the best way to keep out noises, especially if he hummed at the same time.

"You are going to have to wake the kids up George," said Mary Ann to her husband in hushed, urgent tones.

"Whatever for?" George was very tired. He worked all the hours he was offered at the brickyard in order to make the pittance which kept his family in the poor, but honest state they lived in. Christmas Day was his only day off.

"I'm tired. Let the kiddies sleep a bit longer, they will be up soon enough anyway."

He was thinking of the noisy excitement they would enjoy during the day. The few presents he and Mary Ann had managed to get together were hanging in little red stockings above the fireplace downstairs. He did not want the day to start too early.

"The baby's coming George, the baby's coming." Mary Ann tried to keep the panic from her voice. She had already given birth to five children and she was not looking forward to this one.

Labour scared her. She had seen a lot of birth and death in her young life, either attending her family or her friends. There was not always a happy outcome. One of her own babies had died at a young age and she often thought about him.

Especially at Christmas.

George sat up and looked at his wife. She was white and scared and he put his arms around her in comfort. "Alright love, leave it with me. Don't you upset yourself."

He jumped out of bed and put on his trousers. He was already wearing his shirt and underwear and when he threw a jacket on, it meant he was dressed in less than a minute.

The room was freezing cold and he could see his steamy breath in front of his face. Although there would be another hungry mouth and extra responsibility joining their family today, he was looking forward to the birth and quietly prayed for another boy.

He reached across to the window and opened the shabby curtains an inch or two. The glass covered with ice, had formed spidery patterns over the surface. He looked across their little street and could see a lamp lit in the bedroom opposite. John and Lena Monsheimer lived there. They were German, but alright in spite of that. John worked at the timber yard as a labourer and Lena could always be relied upon to help with any birth.

"Georgie!" hissed his dad.

"Yes Dad. What's the matter?" Georgie knew it was Christmas Day and was very excited now he was really awake.

"Get dressed quickly and then get Arthur and your sisters dressed and downstairs."

There was a cry from his mother and Georgie suddenly felt frightened.

"What's the matter with Mum, Dad?" Georgie spoke carefully, his eyes wide with horror.

"We will be getting a new member of the family today Georgie. You are going to have to be a big helping boy." This unaccustomed silliness in the voice of his father unnerved him even more.

"Georgie, do as your Dad says and take your sisters downstairs. You will have to help me and your dad all day today. I am relying on you Georgie love."

Georgie was pleased to hear his mother giving him orders. He loved his mother dearly and was very close to her. He went over to the side of her bed and grabbed her hand.

"Mum, are you alright?"

"Yes my love. Don't you worry. I am just a bit under the weather and will need everyone to help each other today and that will help me."

Georgie felt more comfortable now that he had spoken to his mother. He told his sleepy siblings to get up and he helped them get dressed. They complained and cried, but he soon had them downstairs. Dad had already gone out and by the time the children were downstairs in the kitchen, their Dad was coming back in through the front door.

"Lena will come over soon," he told them.

The children were all excited to hear this news. Lena was always very kind to them.

George began to attend to the range and rattled the poker in the depths of the fire in order to bring it to life. Within a short time, the fire had brightened the room and there was water boiling away in a kettle. Bread was sliced, smeared with dripping and given to the children. They happily waited for their tea. What an exciting Christmas Day this was!

Within half an hour Lena arrived, smiling and carrying a large bag under her arm.

"I've brought some things I think we will be needing," she announced. "I have told Mrs. Horton and she will be along soon."

Georgie listened intently. If Mrs. Horton was coming as well as Lena, then great things must be going on. Mrs. Horton was the very old lady who lived with her husband at the end of Burniston Place. They kept the tobacconist shop which faced onto Elland Road and lived in No 3, which backed onto the shop.

Lena went up the stairs and smiled when she saw her friend crying in pain as she lay on the bed.

"Oh, mein liebling madchen! Lena ist jetzt hier. Alles ist gut."

"I don't think it will be very long Lena, it feels as though it is nearly here."

"A Christmas baby! He will be a blessing to you this child!" said Lena in her cheery way.

"Thank you Lena. I am so glad you are here. But I am very sorry that I am ruining your Christmas Day," said Mary Ann, her voice full of strain.

"Mein liebling, do not cry. We will enjoy the day all the more with all the happy news! Now, Mrs. Horton is on her way. As soon as she comes I shall go downstairs and take die kinder over to our place. Then I will return to help and hold your hand. Everything is ready for Christmas and there will be more than enough food for die kinder today."

"Oh Lena," Mary Ann was crying with gratitude. "I have a chicken in the larder and a pudding which needs steaming. The babies must have their Christmas dinner. What about their presents?"

"George will give the presents to me and they can open them at our house. John will look after everyone. I shall cook your food over here while I am up and down the stairs and if everything is done this afternoon, you can all have your Christmas dinner with the new baby!"

It seemed easy for Lena to arrange all these things for her neighbours, but Lena missed having her own family. She had given birth to six children and not one of them had made it past five years old. She had plenty of love to go around.

There was more commotion downstairs and soon Mrs. Horton had joined the two women in the bedroom. Mrs. Horton had delivered many children locally. She was neither a nurse nor a midwife, but she knew what to do.

She was comfortably off and as her neighbours were all poor, she considered it an act of charity to help where she could. Mrs. Horton was 72 years of age, but did not look it. Her husband was 15 years younger than her and their friends guessed that had something to do with it.

Lena went downstairs and set about her work. As soon as the children were safely across the road and the chicken in the range, she was back upstairs to help bring new Christmas life into the world.

Georgie, Arthur, Annie and Jane were having a great time with Uncle John. He talked in a funny way, but was very kind. Dad had been going back and forth between the two houses and young Georgie was getting very worried about his mother. As the oldest boy, he felt responsible for the other children and the welfare of the family while his parents were so distracted. Dad stayed with them while they opened their presents in front of the fire at Lena and John's. Georgie and Arthur had been happy with their new clothes and a toy each. The outfits had been created by their mother from some second hand clothes she had bought through the church charity. The girls had some hand me down clothes from their cousins, redressed with ribbon bows. They all had sweets, which went down better than the bread and dripping.

Naturally.

Georgie looked out of the window and saw his father walking across the road again, this time with Lena. They came in through the front door and seemed very pleased with themselves.

"Come home children!" he said. "Something very exciting has happened!"

The four children were ready in seconds. They remembered to give a big hug and kiss to Lena and John and clutching their presents followed their father back home.

"Dad it's snowing!" said Annie. Perhaps this is what Dad had meant. They stopped in the middle of the road, heads up, mouths open and eyes wide. Annie thought that the snow looked like fairies jumping out of the sky.

Arthur twirled round, his hands outstretched, looking up into the darkness. He noticed that the snow was sitting on top of the only gas lamp in the street, above number 8 opposite their house. It was all so lovely.

The young Prideaux family arrived back through their own door into the warm room. There was a smell of delicious food and the lamps gave a wonderful glow. The house may be tiny and they were very poor, but none of them wanted to be anywhere else on this magical day.

"Now come on children, your mum wants to see you all upstairs. She has another present for you."

This was news indeed. The children ran up the few steps and as soon as they reached the top step, George picked up his youngest daughter who was almost asleep.

The room seemed darker than usual and there were some funny smells.

"Come on in children," said mum.

Then they saw the surprise. Wrapped in their mum's arms was a new little baby.

"You have a new brother, children. Are you pleased?"

"Is he to keep?" asked Annie.

"Yes."

"Is he Jesus?" asked Jane.

"No Jinny, he isn't. We have not given him a name yet. We can decide now that you are all here."

"Did Jesus send this little boy to take the place of Ben because we all miss him so much?"

Mary Ann looked at George with tears in her eyes. Ben had died on Christmas Eve and had ruined Christmas for the family ever since. He had lain dead in his tiny plank coffin on the table downstairs, while the family waited for there to be enough coffins in the neighbourhood to fill a mass grave at Holbeck. Because of Christmas, Ben was with them for almost a week. Luckily the weather had been very cold. There were some terrible stories of summer deaths and the coffins

19

having to be… Mary Ann didn't want to think of that anymore.

God had sent the perfect remedy.

Georgie saw that his mother looked very tired and drawn, but she seemed happy about the baby. He wondered who had brought it to the house and thought it very bad timing when his mother had been feeling so ill all day.

"Well Dad, what shall we call him?"

Georgie had been named after his father, Arthur after Mary Emma's husband, their uncle. They had looked after George when Mary Emma and George had been orphaned along with their other siblings. Mary Emma and her new husband had taken in the other children in order to save them from the workhouse.

The girls were named in a similarly thoughtful way. Annie, after her mother and Jane after Mary Ann's best friend.

George said, "I have been thinking about this. As you know children, our family used to be very rich and influential. We knew Kings and owned castles and much land before our luck changed. We still have some very rich relatives in Cornwall and Devon. If we visited, they would welcome us with open arms. Never forget that you are all better than the station you currently have in life. Our luck could change back at any moment. Remember that my beautiful children."

Mary Ann did not always approve of this way of talking, but was too tired to stop her husband now. George told anyone who would listen that they were only a couple of generations away from gentry.

"My grandfather and great grandfather were very good friends with Lord Clifford of Chudleigh in Devon. So, in their honour, I would like to call our new son, Clifford."

"Clifford!" said Mary Ann.

"Clifford Prideaux has been born on Christmas Day and is another blessing from God. He has come in place of your beloved brother Ben, who God needed back in heaven to help him. Clifford will bring us luck and all of his family will be special, just like us."

This was a promising speech and the family all beamed at the prospect.

Within an hour, the children were enjoying their second Christmas dinner with mother, father and Clifford in the bedroom. Chicken and potatoes followed by a Christmas pudding. The children never forgot this Christmas Day for the rest of their lives. Not just for the birth of their brother, but because it was the one and only time they were allowed to eat around their parent's bed.

"We should have two Christmas dinners every year!" announced Arthur.

His mother smiled and leant back into the pillows.

"Bedtime, I think," said George.

George had little trouble with the children this bedtime. They quietly snuggled into their little beds and Mary Ann slept heavily while baby Clifford snored lightly in his blanket lined box. Lena and Mrs. Horton had dealt with the soiled sheets and towels by taking them home to their own houses to wash.

Soon after the children had gone to bed, George's brother William knocked quietly on the front door. George opened the door quickly.

"Can I come in please George?"

"Of course you can mate! Come inside, out of the cold. What's the matter?"

William took off his coat and shook the snow from it. His coat was shabby and of doubtful protection against the wintery weather. But poor people are hardened to cold and rarely complain. He took off his thin gloves and placed them onto the now cooling range.

"William, what's the matter?" George put his arm around his brother's shoulders. There was no manly holding back between these brothers. They had been through too much together.

William was crying and sat hunched in the chair by the fire.

It was a full ten minutes before George could get any sense from him.

"Lily has had the baby today. We called him William, but he is too early and he is deformed and the doctor says he won't last very long."

"Oh, William that is terrible news. I am so sorry. How is Lily? She must be devastated."

This boy was the ninth child for William and Lily. Five had already died. Two of them this year alone and to lose yet another child would be heartbreaking for them. But it was just so terrifyingly common amongst the family and friends they both knew.

"William, I don't know what to say." George decided not to mention his new arrival and hoped that nothing would give him away while William was so upset.

If they had money and proper food and housing and doctors that were any good, things would be different. But it was as it was and that was that. The two brothers had already seen so much death and sadness in their lives. They were almost numb to it. George thought again of his son Ben, dead these three years at only one year old.

"Why is life so hard George? Ever since we were born, it's been hard," sobbed William.

"I know," said George. "We are supposed to be grateful for what we have."

"Well some days that's too hard," William answered.

George handed over a whisky and said nothing else to his brother.

*

"What happened to William's little boy, Grandad?" asked Ann.

Clifford was telling his granddaughter about his first Christmas. Although only 5 years old, she listened to everything her beloved grandad told her. It was Christmas Eve 1962 and the family was together for a few days. The two of them stayed with each other as much as possible on these visits and Clifford told her the history of the family and showed her books and documents which she would treasure her whole life.

On this particular afternoon, her mother and siblings were in the same room, but were busy with decorations and sweets. Grandma Agnes came in and out with mince pies and instructions. The others listened only intermittently to the storytelling.

"It wasn't just William. We all had a horrid time. We weren't spoiled rotten like you little girl." Ann wriggled and giggled as he tickled her tummy.

Her mother looked up from her busyness and smiled.

"Tell me Grandad," Ann ordered.

"Uncle William and Auntie Lily had a baby son on that same Christmas Day, but he died on New Year's Eve."

"Did lots of babies die in the olden days?"

"Yes, and people too."

"Why does Jesus want all the people back?"

"He doesn't. We can all go when we want to go. The whole world is just a dream. You have dreams don't you Ann?"

"Yes."

"Well being alive is a dream too. You think up where you want to go and what you want to be and imagine yourself already there. Then one day you will be."

"Like magic?"

"Like magic."

"What happened next?"

"The years passed and there were three further additions to our family. Three more brothers for me, called Herbert, Albert and Wilfred. A larger house was required and the family eventually moved. The nine Prideauxs arrived at 100 Elland Road with great anticipation.

This house was exciting to the children because there was so much more room than at Burniston. Stepping in from the street still brought visitors directly into the room, but it was a lot bigger. This front room had a range topped by a large high mantelpiece which had velvet trimming with long fringes hanging from it. There were ornaments and pots and pans stacked on it. The range had a fender in front which had a seat at each corner. There was a door at the back of the room which led to the cellar. At the top of the cellar stairs were some shelves, one of which was made of marble.

On this slab Mary Ann placed butter, milk and anything which was likely to go off. The upward stairs led to two rooms where the family slept. George and Mary Ann had the tiny room at the back. The boys and girls shared the larger front room which was separated by a curtain.

The toilets were accessed by going out of the front door, walking along the pavement before turning right at the Thrift shop at the end of the street and immediately right into Tilbury Avenue. The toilets were along there."

"What if you wanted to wee right now?" asked Ann.

"We used the potty!"

Agnes pulled a face at her husband. The subject of weeing and potties was bordering on forbidden territory. The other children put hands to mouths and giggled. They had managed to hear this part of the story.

Clifford continued, "At the front of the house on Elland Road were the tracks for the tram, which ran into town or up Elland Road. The tram seat backs could be pushed to either side of the seat depending on which way the tram was travelling. Passengers like to travel forwards, not backwards. Directly opposite the house was the entry to Cemetery Road. That was a creepy walk if we went walking there when it was dark. We used to think a monster lived there. We called him Shudder.

At this new house the family managed to get through the years happily together. Georgie and Arthur fought for their country during the Great War and came home safely although the experience changed them a lot. I missed joining up because I was only 16 years old at the end of the war. Instead I worked at the same brickyard as my father on Claypit Lane. It was a horrible job, but was apparently honest work, my mother said. I thought it was the most boring job in the whole world. Well, I thought that until I got my last job. You make sure that you get a job you like doing, young Ann. Not a boring one."

Ann nodded, her thumb going into her mouth.

"When my sister Annie married Arthur Askin and moved next door to number 98, it suited us all perfectly. Annie wanted to get married, but loved us all so dearly that she could not bear to be parted from us. She offered to help our mother with the ironing and soon was doing all her family's ironing as well as her own. That meant that she washed 36 shirts every Tuesday, 14 of them belonging to me. I insisted on wearing a clean shirt every day for work and another one every evening and I even changed my shirt on Sundays.

She hung the shirts around her house on Tuesday when she took her lunch hour and Mary Ann and Annie ironed them all on Wednesday."

"You said I was spoilt. You were spoilt," said Ann.

Her grandad laughed.

"I used to take Annie's daughter Mary into Leeds and she loved it when the tram driver let her move the back of the seats to face forward. That gave her mum a break."

"Were you very dirty Grandad?"

"No, I wasn't dirty. It was just that the girls all used to chase me and I wanted to look nice. Not like a tramp! I lived at my mum's house until I met your grandma, didn't I Agnes?"

Agnes, who had walked into the room said nothing, but did nod her head in agreement at her husband.

"All the girls found me irresistible, but I was very choosy and only went out with the pretty ones. And when I saw your grandma, I had eyes for no one else and married her as soon as I could."

"When did you get married?"

"Christmas, well as near to Christmas as they would let us. We got married on the 22nd on a Saturday because we weren't allowed to marry on the Sunday or Christmas Eve or Christmas Day. That was bad luck because I like to make Christmas Day the best day for everything."

"What about this Christmas Day?" asked Ann.

"I don't know what special thing will happen this Christmas Day," he answered.

"Its only tomorrow, so we had better think of something quick!" said Ann.

"It's snowing!" shrieked the children.

Everyone went up to the window to look. It certainly was snowing. They opened the front door and looked at the snowflakes coming down. The street lamp was reflecting every flake. The snow looked black when it came down and yellow as it hit the lamps.

Clifford smiled. He puffed away at his pipe and thought about all the Christmases he had had. He felt the sudden familiar pain in his stomach which almost made him double over. He wouldn't let anyone see. This was not the first time it had happened and he made a promise to himself that he would see a doctor in the New Year. That weird feeling came over him again and he looked lovingly at his family. Agnes glanced up at him and suddenly her heart hurt.

"Are you alright, Cliff?" she asked quietly.

"Fine love."

He smiled at her.

*

Agnes brought her head out from under the stairs and said. "Cliff, life does not get any easier."

Agnes picked up the cream sandals she had owned for a quarter of a century and checked the piece of newspaper she had carefully inserted in the soles to cover the hole. "They will do for another year," she said, to no one in particular.

She moved slowly across the hallway and up the stairs. The hallway was freezing cold and dark. Agnes believed in saving money for a possible future need. The hall contained only a small wooden table which housed a bowl contain two bananas and an apple. There was also a black and white photograph in a frame of her two daughters, Dorothy and Ann. On the wall was a small mirror next to which there was a clothes brush. This brush had been used on many occasions by Clifford and their two children when they had lived there together all those years ago.

The mat covered a very small area of the floor and offered little comfort. At the bottom of the stairs was an old vacuum cleaner. It was brown and had a bulbous base. It made a horrifying noise when operated, as though hundreds of ball bearings were being shaken up. It was also almost useless and for that reason was rarely used. There were coats hanging on the hooks at the bottom of the stairs. A blue mac, a light jacket and an overcoat.

Agnes walked up the stairs, carefully holding onto the banister. Everywhere was painted brown in order to not show the dirt. Clifford had decorated the house when they moved here in 1955 and now at Christmas Eve 1993, nothing had changed. The carpet and the paintwork and wallpaper were exactly the same. The lino which was laid everywhere upstairs was of a green and brown mix, but covered in rips and holes. Agnes had put pieces of newspaper under all the rips. Upstairs was as cold as downstairs, but Agnes did not really notice it. The toilet was directly opposite the stairway and was a black and white unit with a high wall mounted cistern and pull chain. The toilet paper was medicated Izal which annoyed her grandchildren intensely.   They could not understand why she did not use soft paper. The bathroom was tiled black and white and in her grandchildren's memories had never had hot water running from the taps, only cold. Any hot water had been carried upstairs from the stove in the kitchen.

The front bedroom contained two beds and had belonged to her daughters until they left home. After that the grandchildren topped and tailed whenever they stayed during their childhood.

Her and Clifford's bedroom was at the back and contained walnut furniture topped with old photographs and ornaments. The wardrobe housed beautiful dresses and a fur stole that no one living had ever seen her wear. Agnes stopped dressing herself up during the summer of 1963.

She sat on the edge of the bed and looked at the small alarm clock on the chest of drawers. It was three in the afternoon and outside was getting dark already. She had nothing to do and no one cared whether she did it or not. Agnes did everything as slowly as possible during the day in order to fill in the hours. Soon she would go downstairs and think about making herself some toast.

It hadn't always been like this though.

Agnes Stones was born in 1911 in a small house in the pit town of South Kirby. Her parents, Mary Lizzie and George lived on the same street and their fathers both worked down the mines. Mary Lizzie became pregnant with their first son when she was fifteen and she and George married when she was sixteen. They lived with Mary's parents in Sheffield and they soon had another son called George. Shortly after this they moved to South Kirby to be near her uncle and his family and Agnes was born. They moved again to Sheffield and Dorothy was born.

As soon as the Great War started George, his friends and relatives all joined up with the fervour that was around at that time. 'Over by Christmas' was the cry as they all marched off to do their bit. Pregnant Mary Lizzie, holding four children was not so impressed.

Two years later George was dead. Shot in the head.

Now the children had to grow up very quickly. Their mother left early for work and the children stayed with their grandmother and sister in-law, who had also lost her husband.

Agnes at four knew what work was. She also knew what doing without and living in extreme poverty was all about. The mice which ran across the bedroom and ate the family's food, gave her a rodent phobia for the rest of her life.

Her mother soon had another relationship which resulted in a daughter she named Nellie. The relationship foundered and she met a painter and decorator who was the father of five children. He was a widower, following his wife's death from Spanish Flu. Mary Lizzie thought John would be a good bet and they soon married and had two further children. Now there were thirteen children and two adults all living in the same house. They all worked very hard trying to feed the whole family and pay the rent. The oldest boys worked in the mines and Agnes worked hard in the home. She did the baking, washing and cleaning and looked after all the children that Mary Lizzie kept bringing into the world.

Before long, the stepfather died and left her with nothing but debts and children. His first litter of children were sent to live with various relations while the other eight remained with Mary Lizzie.

What a life.

14 year old Agnes continued working at home and also went out to work as a tailoress in order to bring in extra money. The boys were still working down the mine.

In spite of this, the house was lively and generally happy. They had trips to Blackpool and Scarborough and bought clothes 'on tick '. The latest fashions and many boyfriends meant that the very attractive girls enjoyed their lives to the full.

Agnes looked at herself in the mirror of her dressing table. She kept the curtains closed because she did not like any neighbours to see what she was doing. With the lights off it was hard to see her face clearly in the glass, so she turned on the bedside light. Clifford had bought her this lamp with its lovely red shade. It was an old fashioned type with brown cord and not recommended for safe use these days, but she did not care. She looked at her face which was still strong and attractive, if a little thin. Her hair was thick and had only become grey in recent years. Her glasses emphasised her dark eyes. She wore a blue checked dress and a blue cardigan.

Her children and grandchildren would recognise this outfit as being one she had worn for many years. Her summer outfits of brightly coloured dresses and green cardigan were similarly recognisable. She had been a beautiful young woman and if she had been given a different life, would have been able to launch a thousand ships of her own.

Clifford had fallen in love with her as soon as he saw her.

Agnes smiled as she looked into the mirror. She could see the reflection of Clifford sitting on the bed. He was smiling at her and she smiled back. When he died in their bed 30 years ago, they had held hands. He had not been the same man after he had been blown up during the war. The irony was that a bomb had gone off in Leeds while he was on leave and blown a wall onto him. He wasn't discovered for over a day and the delay meant he was late rejoining his unit and was marked AWOL. On his return to active duty, with only a small reprimand, he went through D Day and the rest of the fighting unscathed. Although Clifford was not a particularly religious man, just before he died he had sat bolt upright in the bed staring in wonder at the same place

Agnes now sat and said, "Jesus!" Then he smiled and fell back stone dead.

Having no telephone of their own, Agnes had to leave her husband and run a quarter of a mile to the end of the road and ring for help. It seemed like only yesterday.

Agnes got up from the chair and walked back to the bedroom door. It was now quite dark outside and anyone else would have turned on their own lights. Agnes however, did not. Electricity cost money and she knew her way well enough around her home and so there was no real need for lights. Agnes did very little for her own pleasure.

She made her way down the dark stairs, across the hall and into the sitting room. She closed the curtains at either end of the room and thought about lighting the fire, but decided against it. Not much point now.

The room was crowded with furniture. At one end was a table around which her family had sat in the days they lived at home. It had also been the place where many meals were eaten when the grandchildren were quite young. They enjoyed their big family Christmas dinner around it. Nowadays, the family never visited. On the oak side board were the same ornaments which there had always been. There was a large standard lamp, a piano, a gramophone, a sofa and two fire side chairs. The black and white television set had been a gift from her son in law, but was only watched when she had a visitor. The décor was mainly 1950's shabby chic.

Agnes sat down quietly in the chair next to the fire place. She saw her long dead husband sitting in the chair on the other side. He picked up the pipe, filled it with tobacco and spent the next few minutes trying to get it to light. Agnes had been annoyed by this habit when he was alive, but felt comforted by it now. She closed her eyes as she leaned back and remembered the exciting Christmases when her daughters and grandchildren stayed. It was almost as though they were happening right now. She recognised the sounds and the smells.

Agnes got up from the chair, squeezed her husband on the shoulder and left the room. She stood in the hallway for a short time and listened to the noise outside. The children next door must be coming home from school. No, not school, it's Christmas Eve. The letterbox rattled and a card fell on the mat. Agnes picked it up,

"Not even for me. They have either put on the wrong name or put it through the wrong door."

Agnes knew that the neighbours thought she was strange but she did not care. She stopped caring years ago about what people thought of her.

She walked into the kitchen. This tiny room was marginally warmer than the rest of the house and if she lit the cast iron stove, it would be very warm and cosy. But she could not remember the last time the stove had been lit. There was little point these days with only Agnes at the house and it seemed such a lot of work and fuss for only one person. The coal house was full of the coal which had been ordered and delivered in 1988, but no visitors meant that there was no one to fuss over and so the coal was never used. She looked at the old gas cooker which stood behind the enamel table and remembered that she wanted a cup of tea. She filled the kettle with a small amount of water, struck a match and turned on the gas. The stove would have been condemned years previously had anyone ever been called in to check it out. After an alarming flash, the gas was lit and the kettle began to heat up. The sink, of the old enamel variety contained a metal bowl which served as a washing up bowl. Agnes took a cup and saucer from the wooden draining board, took the teapot from the table and placed a spoon of tea inside. Soon the kettle began to whistle and Agnes poured the boiling water into the teapot and waited for it to mash. She dripped a small amount of milk into the cup and poured a thin stream of weak tea into that. Agnes knew she should eat something and opened the pantry door. Inside at the back she could see twenty bags of flour, at least the same of sugar, five large packets of cornflakes, ten jars of mincemeat, four pounds of butter and some marmalade. In front of this there was a loaf of bread and some cheese. She took the loaf and one of the packets of butter and made herself a cheese sandwich.

Agnes sat down at the table and began her meal.

Meeting and marrying Clifford was one of the best things that happened to her. Agnes enjoyed having a handsome husband and a nice house round the corner from her mother and her married siblings. When their first daughter arrived they were thrilled and when Agnes was pregnant for a second time they looked forward to the birth of a son. Then war broke out in September 1939 and Clifford joined up, much to the horror of Agnes. Her handsome husband left her, she gave birth to a disappointing second daughter and Clifford rarely returned to their home until 1947. He had decided to stay on in order to help remove mines. Agnes let part of the house to serving soldiers in order to make extra income. Clifford returned looking much older and slightly weakened by his experience and their marriage was never the same again.

They both tried very hard to make their marriage work and after a few months managed to make some sort of a relationship. Of course, almost as soon as they settled back into a normal existence where Clifford left the house at six every morning to work as a stonemason, the rumours started about the houses in which they lived were to be demolished. Agnes's mother married a single neighbour called Herbert, in order that they could get a council house as a married couple. As single people they stood little chance. Herbert was very sweet and caused Mary Lizzie no trouble at all. At the same time, Agnes and Clifford moved to this lovely little cottage in Bramley.

After Clifford died, Agnes wondered if her life was ever going to be nice again. It seemed that she had had so little happiness in life. She had no faith in God, since he had taken away everyone she loved and no matter how hard she worked, she had saved very little money. Still, here she was, 82 years of age, lonely, cold and miserable.

Thank you God.

Agnes could hear noises in the sitting room again. It sounded like people talking, but of course it couldn't be so. She ignored it. Soon she could hear noises upstairs, the sound of running water and voices. She ignored this too.

This had been happening for many years and Agnes assumed that she was just remembering the visitors she used to have. She was probably projecting the memory into her house.

Agnes got up from the chair and went to the cupboard which was crammed full of old newspapers and Beano comics. There was a special smell every time this cupboard was opened. It was a sort of mouldy smell. She took out one of the newspapers and paid little attention to the date on the front of the paper, the 14th of June 1969. News doesn't change that much, just the characters. She spread the newspaper on the table, read it for a while and carefully folded it up and put it back in the cupboard. That will do for tonight.

She looked at the kitchen clock. It said seven o'clock, time for bed.

She made her way upstairs, walking quite slowly. She used the bathroom as usual and made her way into the bedroom. She changed quickly into her voluminous nightie and climbed into bed. No lights and no heating, Agnes was used to living like this. Her life was very quiet.

As a young girl, there was noise everywhere. The house was constantly busy. So many people living in such a small space meant that even the children were aware of their parent's intimate moments together. There were children crying, pots boiling and the seemingly permanent loud voice of her mother. It was also possible to hear the neighbour's lives through the walls. Those houses were built back to back and there were no yards. The front door led straight onto the street, which everyone in the neighbourhood used as a communal area. Washing hung in the street on lines going from one house to another. There were no secrets to be kept there. Everyone knew if a husband came back drunk or indeed whether he came back at all. They knew whose children were causing trouble and would have no qualms about clouting them without the need to call in a policeman. Agnes had hated all of the neighbourly intrusion and with that memory had become quite secretive once she had a family of her own. By the time she was widowed, Agnes lived almost as a hermit. She could leave the house and go for two weeks holiday without any neighbour knowing she had left. She began to do work in the garden at dusk or very early in the morning in order that she was not seen by anyone else.

One of her earliest memories was her mother giving birth with grandmother and the woman from down the road in attendance. When the last three girls were born, Agnes helped in the delivery. This experience paid off later on in her life when she helped her own girls give birth in this very cottage. It was such a pity that Agnes did not see them so much now. A person becomes involved so deeply with their own family and when they grow and move away it just seems unfair. She didn't like to think of it too much, because it was really quite cruel that none of her family came to visit her. It was Christmas Day tomorrow and she knew there would no family or friends arriving. Agnes wondered why her granddaughter Ann never came now. So heartless.

Agnes lay down in the bed. She still slept on her side of the bed. She had only shared her sleeping quarters since Clifford's death with her grandchildren when they were very young. It did not even enter her head to sleep in the middle of the bed and spread out like a star fish.

Now, listen, there were the noises again and the voices. They seemed to be in the same room as her, but that could not be so. It must be the children next door making too much noise and the sound of their voices was travelling through the dividing wall. Agnes thought she could hear the television on. There was plenty of music and the dull boom, boom, boom of some kind of tune. Agnes thought about complaining, but the last time she had gone round and knocked on their door, she had been completely ignored. She thought she had been speaking quite calmly, but the family carried on talking amongst themselves until Agnes had decided to leave. Once she had walked all the way into Leeds and into the council offices to complain about the noise and the staff had taken no notice of her. It seemed that now she was getting older, she was becoming invisible. When a person is young and vital everyone pays attention. When she was young and beautiful there was nowhere she went where people did not turn to look at her. Was it just the simple fact that older people are overlooked or was it that people did not want to be associated with her? Agnes could not work this out, it just made her feel very sad and angry.

46

She thought about her own mother and could not recall her ever having been ignored.   Mary Lizzie was always so loud that people had to take notice of her. Agnes sometimes wished she could be more like that, but she knew she could not.

"Is there anybody there?"

Agnes sat upright. She was sure that she had heard those words correctly.

The voices seemed to be coming from her sitting room. Should she go downstairs? What if there really was someone there? What would she do about it?

No, this was getting ridiculous, she would go downstairs. She swung her legs over the side of the bed and into her warm slippers. She put her shawl around her shoulders for the sake of modesty and quietly opened the bedroom door. The rest of the house was in darkness and she made her way down the stairs feeling her heart beating almost out of her chest. She quietly opened the sitting room door and looked around the edge of it to see if anyone was there.

There were people seated around her table.

It was dark in the room, save for some candles on the table and on the sideboard. There was a funny smell in the air of a sort of smoky perfume.

What on earth were they doing in her sitting room? The shock of seeing the intruders emboldened Agnes and she moved into the room and across the floor. The strangers around the table turned to stare at her and one of the women began to scream. The woman sitting next to the screamer held her arm and told her to be quiet. A man who appeared to be in charge of the group, looked at Agnes and asked her if she wanted any help.

Agnes did not answer. Why where these people in her house and asking her if she needed help? Agnes could not understand this, it was a bad dream. She turned, intent on leaving the room and the house and fetching some help.

"No don't leave," said the man. "We don't mean you any harm. Do you mean us harm?"

This was crazy. Agnes could not understand what he was talking about and why he was asking such stupid questions.

"Is that you Agnes?" asked one of the women. "I've come to talk to you."

"Why didn't you just come during the daytime?" said Agnes. She really must be dreaming.

"We have come to help you move," said Grace. "Come and sit down with us."

"I'm quite happy where I am," answered Agnes. "I don't want to move. My daughters have tried to get me into those places before, but I refused to go. And I am not going now."

"She said that she doesn't want to leave and that she's quite happy here," the man told the others.

"But she can't be happy all on her own here. Come on Agnes, we'll help you see your husband again. Look behind you, can you see him there?"

Agnes turned around and saw Clifford sitting in his chair by the fire, smoking his pipe. Clifford smiled and held out his arms to her.

Agnes noticed that he had lit the fire and she went over to him and sat on the arm of his chair. She felt 30 years old again. She laughed and noticed how the room filled with light. The Christmas tree was up and the children and grandchildren were sitting around the room. There was food on the table and drinks on the sideboard. It was all as it should be. She must have fallen asleep after Christmas dinner and had a horrid dream. She jumped up, brushed down her beautiful dress and went into the kitchen to fetch some more food.

"Hurry up Aggie! I'm missing you already!" shouted Clifford.

He smiled at his granddaughter and said, "I told you, it's all just a dream."

Ann nodded and replied, "I understand now Grandad."

*

"Well, that went better than I thought it would. Everything should be all right now," Grace said to the others around the table.

"She looked like a proper ghost floating in the room all dressed in white. People won't believe that really happened," said the man.

"We know it did though. She is with her husband now, so he will look after her."

"The owners of this place should be much happier without Agnes walking about the house in her nightie all the time. They have been really creeped out about it. They have been seeing her for years."

"I don't know why they should be scared, she seemed like a really nice lady." said another.

"Apparently lights were being turned off and taps turned on when there was no one to be seen."

"And it was cold all the time, no matter whether the heating was on or not."

"They kept seeing a grey lady floating about the place. Agnes lived here for years by herself before she died in 1988. She was starting to get a little confused in the months before she died, so probably didn't notice that she had actually died. That happens quite a lot."

They blew out the candles, turned on the main light and walked out of the house into the snowy Christmas Eve.

FOOTNOTES

- Clifford Prideaux (1902-1963) was my grandfather and is the latest subject of my historical short stories.

- He was born and lived as I have described in the story.

- I was either told the details of this story by Clifford and my mother or in later years by descendants of his siblings.

- His brother William did have a baby that same Christmas Day, he died of his problems soon after.

- Christmas features more than you would think in the Prideaux history.

- The story of the coffin on the kitchen table was told to me by Annie's daughter.

- She told me the tale of the shirt ironing. As a young girl she was involved in the washing and ironing. She also helped in the preparations for the street party to celebrate Clifford and Agnes's wedding. She was allowed to attend as a reward.

- She also told me about the layout of Elland Road. This was demolished years ago.
- Photographs of Burniston Place and other properties can be found on the Leodis website here. The house was demolished years ago.
- Clifford died on 8th September 1963 of acute intestinal obstruction and adhesions. The cause was put down to the bombing he suffered during the war. He was only given a cursory checkup and sent back to the fighting. The fact he had lain underneath a fallen wall for almost a day, did not warrant further investigation. Hindsight meant that the pain he had been suffering from had been severe ever since the bombing.
- The death bed scene where Clifford said 'Jesus' and died, did happen. It was talked about in the family for a long time afterwards. Grandma locked the doors when he died before she ran to the phone. She didn't want him to be stolen.

- Agnes's life was far more interesting than I have given it credit here.
- Clifford passed on stories, documents and histories to me about the Prideaux family. These had been handed down to him. I wish that I could ask him more questions now. But I can't because he is dead.
- Agnes remained at the cottage until her death on 14th February 1988. She did become a little vague towards the end of her life. Obviously it was because she was beginning to see Clifford again...
- I used the cottage as Gran Prix's house in Shudder.
- There are many descendants of Clifford's Prideaux siblings in Yorkshire and all around the world. I am in contact with quite a few.

A SELECTION OF PUBLICATIONS

OF

PAGANUS PUBLISHING

Shudder by A A Prideaux.

Who or what is Shudder?

The Old Mill was the place in Mill Town where most people worked. Years passed and the mill closed, but something remained inside. The townspeople had ignored the missing children and the frightening stories of devils and ghosts for as long as they could remember. It was easier to carry on and accept the money the Snooty family provided in return for working at the mill. Everyone allowed the Council members to run their lives and control their ideas without question. Questions were always ignored and the questioner punished. When Lydia Prix returned to the town after her marriage failed, she had no choice but to face the demons of the past and ultimately face the truth. The town would never be the same again. If you go down to the woods today, you may end up being frightened of more than you think...

The Specials by A A Prideaux is a murder mystery set in 2012.

An old man is found dead in his home and DCI Revie and DS Jackson face the task of discovering who murdered him. At first, it appears that there is no reason the quiet widower should have been killed. But the investigation soon reveals that the gentle old man had been a long term and particularly deviant paedophile. As the story unfolds throughout the year and the body count rises, the police discover more people who have been living an apparently normal life while successfully hiding their past. The lives of all the people involved can never be the same again.

The Specials reaches its dramatic conclusion in Snowdonia.

A Ghost Story by A A Prideaux stars John Prideaux (1505-1568) lived in Stowford and had a wife and two children. He had lots of friends and great connections and lived in one of the largest houses in Stowford.

One evening in 1547, he and his family and friends were at their usual Tuesday night dinner. They took weekly turns as to which house the dinner and entertainment were held. This night was the turn of the Prideaux family at Stowford Manor. They ate their meal and as they settled down, John told the gathering a ghost story. He told them of a stranger he once befriended and the mysterious path the meeting led him along. Present at the dinner were Parson William Hele, Robert and Sybil Fox, Thomas and Joan Rogers and John and Ann Prideaux. Before the evening ended, the friends are on a mysterious quest of their own, leading to a remarkable conclusion at St Petrocs church on snowy Dartmoor.

The story of '**The Bishop and the Witch' by A A Prideaux**
takes place between 1596 and 1608.John Prideaux was born
near Dartmoor in 1578 and eventually became Bishop of
Worcester. He spent most of his adult life at Exeter College,
Oxford as Regius Professor and Vice Chancellor.

He was involved in many of the important events which took
place in England during the reigns of Elizabeth I, James I and
Charles I.

When John Prideaux gave evidence in 1606 at the Star
Chamber about Anne Gunter, he did so as a well-known and
respected Oxford academic.

At the 1604 Witch Trial at Abingdon her alleged tormentors,
Elizabeth Gregory, Agnes and Mary Pepwell were ultimately
found to be innocent. Anne was sent to stay with Henry
Cotton, the Bishop of Salisbury until her father confronted the
King and asked him to intervene in the bewitching case.

King James took a personal interest in Anne's troubles and put
her under the control of Richard Bancroft, the Archbishop
of Canterbury. Anne later confessed to King James that her
symptoms were faked on the instructions of her father, Brian
Gunter. He was arrested and faced his accusers at the Star
Chamber in 1606.

Anne Gunter was given a dowry by King James and she disappeared from the history books. History does not tell us what happened to Anne Gunter, but A A Prideaux provides us with a potential solution.

A A Prideaux tells the story of the possible meeting of John Prideaux and Anne Gunter at a much earlier time and how that meeting could have had a bearing on the outcome of the trial. Most of the characters playing a part in this story actually existed, making her version of events a possible one.

"John and Anne become friends and allies and we find that the story was not such a simple one. We discover who the real witches were and how John struggled with his faith during his involvement with the Gunter family. The reader must draw their own conclusions whether the events were caused by demons or drugs. This is an alternative tale based on historical facts and a lot of artistic license."

A A Prideaux

THANK YOU. DO CALL AGAIN.